THE MUMMY'S CURSE

BY CATHERINE CHAMBERS

LONDON, NEW YORK, MUNICH,
MELBOURNE, AND DELHI

DK LONDON
Series Editor Deborah Lock
Project Editor Camilla Gersh
Project Art Editor Hoa Luc
US Senior Editor Shannon Beatty
Producer, Pre-production Francesca Wardell
Illustrator Emmanuel Cerisier

DK DELHI
Editor Nandini Gupta
Assistant Art Editor Tanvi Nathyal
DTP Designers Anita Yadav, Vijay Kandwal
Picture Researcher Sakshi Saluja
Deputy Managing Editor
Soma B. Chowdhury

Reading Consultant
Dr. Linda Gambrell, Ph.D.

First American Edition, 2014

Published in the United States by
DK Publishing
345 Hudson Street, 4th Floor
New York, New York 10014

14 15 16 17 18 10 9 8 7 6 5 4 3 2 1

001—256513—August/14

Published in Great Britain by Dorling Kindersley Limited

A catalog record for this book is available from the Library of Congress

ISBN: 978-1-4654-1971-2 (pb)
ISBN: 978-1-4654-1972-9 (hc)
Printed and bound in China by South China Printing Co., Ltd.

DK books are available at special discounts when purchased in bulk for sales promotions, premiums, fund-raising, or educational use. For details, contact: DK Publishing Special Markets, 345 Hudson Street, 4th Floor, New York, New York 10014 or SpecialSales@dk.com.

Discover more at.
www.dk.com

CONTENTS

4   Meet the Members

6   The Location

8   Prologue

16   **Chapter 1** The Curse of the Flood

32   **Chapter 2** The Curse of Seth

46   **Chapter 3** The Curse of the Nile

60   **Chapter 4** The Curse of the Poor

74   **Chapter 5** The Curse of the Celebrity Chef

86   **Chapter 6** The Curse of the Priest

102   **Chapter 7** The Curse of the Mummy

118   Epilogue

122   The Mummy's Curse Quiz

124   Glossary

126   Index

127   About the Author and Consultant

MEET THE MEMBERS

Imagine that, in a split second, you could be transported to a museum or historical site anywhere on the planet. Well, a group of young history enthusiasts turned the dream into reality, creating a unique club called Secretly Living in the Past (SLIP). One of its members, Seth, developed a cell phone app that took the members to museums and historical sites all over the world. Then he made a terrible, but wonderful, mistake! His app now tumbles SLIP members back into the time period of their choice to face history as it happened. That is anywhere and whenever they wish...

SECRETLY
LIVING
IN THE
PAST

SETH: in Cornwall, England. He is an app expert and inventor. He discovered, purely by accident, how to SLIP into the past, and took part in the very first expedition to ancient Rome.

MUSA: in Cairo, Egypt. He is an eager Egyptologist. His family have worked alongside archaeologists in Egypt for decades. They have made many discoveries.

ABRINET: in Axum, northern Ethiopia. She is the heroine of the first expedition. She is also interested in ancient Nubia, which developed south of ancient Egypt.

HIROTO: in Kyoto, Japan. He is passionate about ancient languages. He has developed a translator app and was crucial to the success of the first SLIP expedition.

LUANA: in Sao Pedro da Aldeia, Brazil. She studies ancient religions and their followers. She has developed an app that explains the local religions and customs in ancient times.

5

THE LOCATION

In the shadows of ancient Egypt's rocky
hills, the cries and clatter of bustling ports
echo in the desert air. In royal courts,
humble courtyards, and bustling streets,
musicians play, scribes carve poetry
on limestone slabs, and dancers whirl
around the noisy crowds. Towering above
them all, pyramids hide their solemn,
deathly secrets. It is in this era of
majesty and mystery that our
time travelers find themselves...

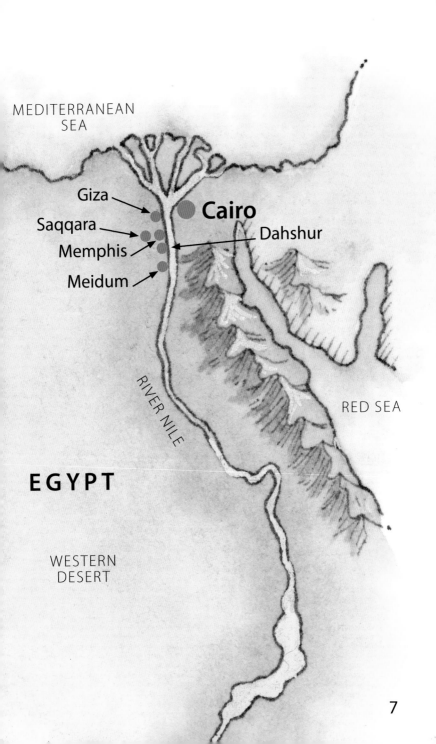

MEDITERRANEAN
SEA

Giza

Saqqara

Memphis

Meidum

Cairo

Dahshur

RIVER NILE

RED SEA

EGYPT

WESTERN
DESERT

7

PROLOGUE

"Want 2 SLIP guys? Destination: Giza—ancient Egypt. Year: 2585BCE. Ruler: King Snefru. SLIP date: Sat, Sept 15. Time: 09:00 GMT."

Musa pressed the send button and then waited impatiently for their replies. He sat down on a steep limestone step to calm himself. It had been uncovered that very day on a new archaeological site, lying not far from the Red Pyramid at Dahshur, now bathed in dusk's crimson light.

What a great find! Musa was so proud that his own father and uncle had discovered it. Beneath the step, a propped-up stone slab covered a jagged entrance, and a steamy, musty-smelling tunnel dipped steeply into the darkness below. It would take the archaeology team months to uncover its secrets, but that made it even more exciting.

"Dahshur!" thought Musa keenly. "It was the reign of King Snefru and the birth of true pyramid-building, when rumors of tomb curses grew to create mystery—and fear. Snefru. What a guy! It's a shame they never found his tomb, nor his wife's. If only they knew what had happened to them."

Musa's cell phone rumbled in his pocket.

"Can come later for a bit. Can add more gods 2 my app. C u! Luana."

"Help, no! Exams! Study! Abrinet."

"Will stay here 2 help u with language problems, as usual! Hiroto."

"WOW! Yeah! ME! ME! ME! Seth."

Musa sighed with relief. Luana was a really great SLIP companion. He was a bit nervous about Seth, though. Although he was a fantastic computer programmer, if anyone could get them into trouble, it was Seth. On the other hand, if anyone could get them out of it again, it was Seth. Musa had to smile.

Musa made his way past the site's guards toward his home. That night, he would listen excitedly to his grandfather's tales

of past digs and discoveries, and of intrigue and unexplained happenings. Was it true that gods and goddesses cursed those who uncovered tombs?

Musa knew that the answers lay deep in Egypt's ancient past. He needed those answers because he had entered the annual National Young Archaeologists' Discovery Competition! Its topic? "The Curse of the Mummies: True or False?" Only a SLIP would give Musa a chance to find out—and to win!

Make Your Own Pyramid

A pyramid is any structure with triangular sides that meet in a point at the top. The Egyptians built huge pyramids, but it is easy to build your own mini pyramids at home.

YOU WILL NEED

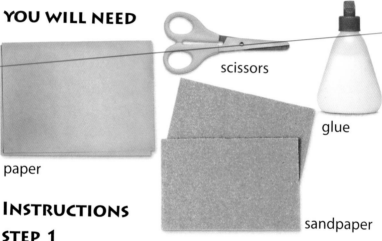

scissors

glue

paper

sandpaper

Instructions

Step 1
Trace the pyramid net, or outline, onto the paper.

Step 2
Cut out the pyramid net.

Step 3
Fold the net along the dotted lines.

Step 4
Glue flap A to side A, flap B to side B, flap C to side C, and flap D to side D. You now have a pyramid!

Step 5
Glue the pyramid down onto the sandpaper.

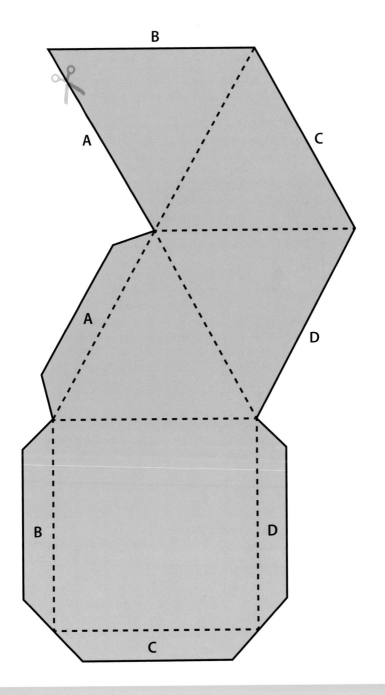

Ancient Egypt Time Line

c2613BCE
Snefru becomes King of Egypt; he is responsible for the construction of the Bent Pyramid at Dahshur.

c1336BCE
Tutankhamun becomes King of Egypt.

c3200BCE
Egyptian hieroglyphs are first used.

c2181BCE
King Pepi II dies, beginning a period of civil war in Egypt.

c3000BCE   c2500BCE   c2000BCE   c1500BCE

Early Dynastic Period (c3100–c2686BCE)

Old Kingdom (c2686–c2181BCE)

Middle Kingdom (c2040–c1650BCE)

New Kingdom (c155 c1069

c2667BCE
Djoser becomes King of Egypt; this marks the beginning of a period of large-scale building projects.

c2040BCE
Nebhepetre Mentuhotep of Thebes defeats rivals to unite Egypt and launch the Middle Kingdom period.

c2609BCE
Khufu becomes King of Egypt; it is under his direction that the Great Pyramid of Giza is constructed.

Note:
When historians are not sure of the precise date of something, they write "c" before the year. This stands for "circa," which means "approximately."

c332BCE
Alexander the Great
conquers Egypt;
his successors
would launch
the Ptolemaic
[taw-le-MAY-ik] dynasty.

c1000BCE	c500BCE	0	c500CE

Ptolemaic Period
(c332–30BCE)

c30BCE
Egypt becomes a province
in the Roman Empire.

c44BCE
Cleopatra VII of the
Ptolemaic Dynasty
becomes Queen of Egypt.

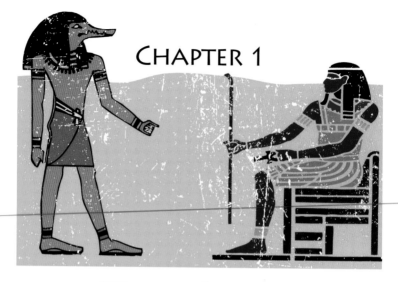

CHAPTER 1

THE CURSE
OF THE FLOOD

Day: Saturday
Date: September 15
Time: 08:59 GMT

"SLIP app synchronizer open?"
texted Seth.

"Open," replied Musa.

"OK. We SLIP."

5-4-3-2-1. Star key—pound-pound-pound.
The mission had begun.

Thirty seconds later, Seth had landed. "BLUUUURGH!" he said, as he stood up in a pool of dark, stinking water, choking.

"We're cursed!" he yelled.

"Stop complaining!" demanded Musa, spitting out a piece of smelly bulrush. "We've made it! Early Giza—where the curses and the blessings of great gods and goddesses really got going!"

Seth looked unconvinced and stared silently around their landing spot in a walled, flooded garden. Some way from the wall stood a grand, two-story house, with its own temple set behind it. It was built high on a river bluff to show its importance and to keep it safe from the annual floodwaters.

The garden was dotted with date palms, doum palms, and fig trees. Rose bushes spattered with mud held firm above a carpet of scented flowers flattened by the floodwaters. Fish that were once confined to a central pond now swam freely around the garden, nibbling at Musa's and Seth's toes.

Musa and Seth had come prepared: they wore linen loincloths and skirts, and long, dark wigs. The murky water left particles of fine, gray silt on their clothes, skin, and

hair. As they shook off the dark drops of water, Musa was reminded what a life-giving combination silt and water were for the Egyptians. Every year, the silt and water washed down from the upper reaches of the Nile in huge torrents, flooding the desert and transforming it into rich, fertile farmland.

Musa pointed to a long funeral procession, snaking its way toward the temple and the sacred Nile beyond.

"Look, Seth! A mummy! It's all laid out
in a beautiful wooden funeral boat, with its
long, snakelike prow. It must be for someone
rich. I can smell the preservatives and
perfumes from here! I can hear the dancers
and musicians. Let's take a look."

"YEH!" A boy leaped off the red-brick
garden wall and pulled Seth and Musa
away toward an arched gate, shouting
at them.

"What's he saying? What's he saying?"
asked Seth.

Musa looked at his cell phone. "Hiroto's
translator takes time. It's not easy to know

what such an ancient language sounds like...
hold on... Khemten. His name's Khemten."

The boy nodded.

"Yes, yes. That's me. C'mon now! Out of
here! Don't even think of joining the funeral
procession! If you touch that mummy,
you could die!"

"It's cursed?" asked Seth.

"No! Don't you know that people are dying
of cholera from these old, diseased pools of
floodwater? The mummy's infected! Even
Ptah, great god of Memphis, can't protect
the rich. Let's head for the river, where the
water's clean and flowing!"

Khemten grabbed hold of Seth's and Musa's arms and ran with them, a twisted foot making him limp slightly. He pulled them through the maze of alleyways, squeezed tightly between the riverside warehouses, until they reached the Nile. The river glided ahead of them like a slowly rippling, glistening mirror. It carried passenger boats, barges, and little papyrus fishing rafts, innocently unaware of the destruction it had recently caused.

"Over there are the pure waters of our sacred river here in Giza. Maybe the god Ptah never leaves it. Maybe that will keep us from getting sick here," said Khemten. "He blesses us workers by the water."

Musa and Seth turned to thank their new friend.

"No, don't thank me. Just tell me who you are. You are strangers, I know—maybe from another world. I have a gift, I am told, that enables me to tell these things."

When they told Khemten their names, he jumped in surprise.

"Seth's the name of an ancient Egyptian god," laughed Musa. "What a coincidence, eh? Just don't get full of yourself!" he said, seeing Seth's smug face. "He's got a seriously ugly face!"

"Well, I must get to work," Khemten said, walking toward a gang of dockworkers loading a barge. "Where are you bound?"

"We're waiting for a friend. Then we're hoping to catch a boat up the Nile toward Memphis—toward the tombs at Dahshur."

"You can stay a while and help, then. You look well fed. You are no doubt princes who know nothing of the work of the poor."

Seth and Musa looked rather uncomfortable as they joined the line of hopeful men and boys. While they waited, they watched tough dockers loading a huge, broad, flat-bottomed barge, hauling huge chunks of limestone quarried nearby onto an empty vessel with thick, flax ropes.

"That stone has been rescued from a damaged barge moored behind it," Khemten said.

Boat-builders were working tirelessly to repair the barge, which was taking in water and listing dangerously to one side.

"They are replacing the broken planks of cedar wood," Khemten continued, "an expensive material used mainly for the king's fleet." Seth and Musa watched as some workers used rulers and triangles to measure up the wood. Then, with great skill, others were cutting the planks using large axes. Next they planed them with small tools used for carving called adzes and smoothed them with abrasive stones. The holes along the planks were being threaded with strong halfah grass and tied together. Still other workers were stuffing papyrus in between the planks to stop water from seeping through.

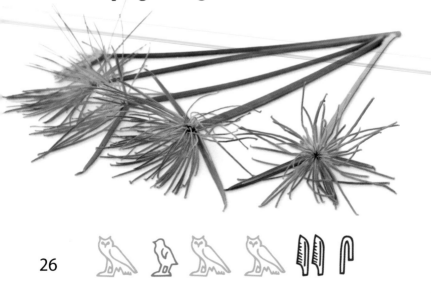

While they were working, Khemten asked the boat-builders for a basket and began collecting the sawdust.

"You don't know what this is for, do you?" he asked Seth and Musa. They shook their heads.

"This sawdust—it's valuable, you know," Khemten explained. "The resin in it keeps insects away, and of course, it's used to stuff mummies, too! Here, take these brooms. We must sweep up all of these droppings from the carrier donkeys on the quayside."

"Oh, NO! Not again! Every SLIP, I have to mess with donkey droppings. I'm CURSED!" grumbled Seth.

?
What does Khemten
say sawdust can
be used for?

Egyptian Gods

The ancient Egyptians had more than 2,000 gods who ruled over every aspect of their lives.

Amun-Ra: creator god ↑
He was represented as a man wearing a crown with two feathers.

←Seth: god of violence and the desert He was depicted with the head of an unknown creature.

Osiris: god of the dead →
He was shown as a mummy wearing a crown.

←Hapi: god of the Nile
He was shown as a man with a large belly wearing a crown made of lotus or papyrus.

↑ Sekhmet: goddess of war She had the head of a lioness so also represented cats.

←Ptah: god of the arts He was usually depicted as a mummy holding a scepter.

Isis: goddess of → magic and life She was represented as a woman.

←Wadjet-Bast: protectress of Lower Egypt When Wadjet was represented with the head of a cat, she became Wadjet-Bast.

THE FLOODING OF THE NILE

Egypt is an area that gets very little rain. Hence people in ancient Egypt relied on the flooding of the Nile River, which occurred at around the same time every year, to ensure that their crops got enough water.

UPPER COURSE

Sometimes the water flows from the mountains in the form of waterfalls.

MIDDLE COURSE

The floodplain is flooded when the river overflows its banks.

LOWER COURSE

A delta is a huge fan-shaped area composed of silt.

WHY THE NILE FLOODED

In about early June, heavy rain and melting snow begin to flow down the Nile River from the mountains in Ethiopia, bringing tiny bits of rock down from the hills with it. In ancient Egypt, this caused the river to flood. When the floodwater stopped flowing and then receded, it left the tiny bits of rock behind, forming a fine, new soil called silt. This soil was very fertile—ideal for growing crops. The most fertile soil was found in the Nile Delta, which is where the river meets the sea. Today, the flooding of the Nile is controlled by a dam in Aswan in the south of Egypt.

GODS AND STARS

The ancient Egyptians believed that the flowing of the river from the mountains was actually the coming of the god Hapi. They also noticed that the star Sirius rose just before the Nile flooding, so they could predict when the flooding was going to start. They believed that this star was the goddess Isis and that the flowing of the Nile was the tears she shed over the death of her husband Osiris.

The star Sirius next to the constellation Orion.

THE EGYPTIAN CALENDAR

Since the flooding of the Nile was so important to the Egyptians, they based their entire calendar on it. The year was divided into three seasons based on when the Nile flooded and when farming could take place. The year was then divided into 12 months, which were numbered according to which season they were in.

Name of the season	Months in the season	Meaning	Modern time of year
Akhet	First of Akhet Second of Akhet Third of Akhet Fourth of Akhet	season of flooding	June to September
Peret	First of Peret Second of Peret Third of Peret Fourth of Peret	season of planting	October to mid-February
Shemu	First of Shemu Second of Shemu Third of Shemu Fourth of Shemu	season of harvesting	mid-February to May

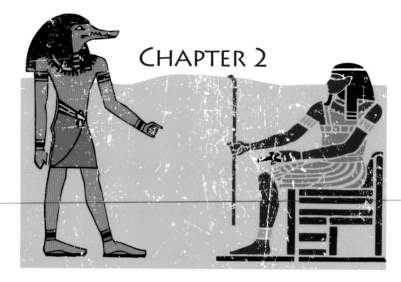

CHAPTER 2

THE CURSE OF SETH

Musa glared at Seth with embarrassment and handed him a broom made of long split reeds tied in a fan shape with papyrus string. Seth screwed up his nose and shoveled the dung quickly into the Nile.

"NOOO!" shouted Khemten. "Are you crazy? I need to sell it! We mix it with straw and clay to make bricks, or dry it for fuel. Herbalists cook medicines with it, and look

here!" Khemten pointed to an amulet in a beetlelike shape hanging around his neck. "Even my amulet is made of dung! It represents the god Khepri, who pushes the sun across the sky the way the beetle pushes dung. Let me offer it to you, Seth, to keep you calm!"

"Ooh. You keep it! I wouldn't want you to be cursed!" Seth replied.

"I don't believe in such things! My uncle gave it to me. It shows I'm cared for, and not a street kid. Do you understand?" Khemten watched as Seth stared at the amulet in disgust. Khemten fell down laughing.

With several full baskets, their work was done, and Khemten was paid with a basketful of his own. He smiled broadly.

"Now I have plenty to sell. It means I'll be able to pay for more lessons with the scribe tutor. I think you two have brought me blessings." Khemten limped away from the river through the maze of alleyways.

A yowl and a voice screaming, "MAU!" put a jarring halt to the rhythms of the dockside. Mau, a cat, was tumbling from the loaded barge toward the river, twisting to try to save herself as she plunged into the inky waters.

"Hold on! I'll save you!" called Seth. Then, as he dove between the boat and the bank, he yelled, "Oh, no! I'm probably polluting the sacred Nile! I'll be cursed!"

However, as Seth rose from the riverbed clutching a dripping cat, the dockers, boat-builders, sailors, and captain, who had yelled, "MAU!" all cheered.

"You've brought good fortune to my boat!" cried the captain. "May Sekhmet shower blessings upon you always!"

"Yaaay! Sekhmet!" chanted the crew.

"Who's Sekhmet?" asked Seth.

"Well, according to Luana's app here, she's a goddess of cats and lions," Musa replied, deftly replacing his cell phone under his wig.

"LUANA!" Seth and Musa looked at each other in sheer panic.

"She'll be landing any minute—at our landing site in that muddy garden near the temple! She won't know how to find us!" cried Musa, getting ready to run.

"There's no way we can go back there!" said Seth. "Remember the curse of cholera!"

"Well, you're the app expert, not me. Do something!" urged Musa.

"I am. I'm resetting the coordinates on the app. She should be with us in 1 minute 40 seconds."

"You're a genius!"

"I know," said Seth, grinning.

Musa and Seth watched anxiously as Luana landed silently and elegantly alongside them on the towpath. She turned to them, wasting no time.

"Seth Trewyn! Those reed sandals you're wearing are really cheap. Why are you wet? Musa! You're covered in gray silt! Gross.

No wonder you always end up having to sell donkey droppings to survive on your SLIPS. You'll have to pretend you're my servants."

Seth blushed—how did she know about the donkey droppings?

"Well, at least we don't make everybody stare!" he retorted.

It was true. Not only did the dockworkers stare, they bowed, for Luana was dressed like an Egyptian princess. A flowing, white-linen dress floated from two shoulder straps down to her ankles, drawn in at the waist with a silver belt. A long, pleated shawl covered her shoulders, and she positively dripped with gold, her bracelets, necklace, and rings all decorated with semi-precious stones.

Seth and Musa sighed. It was great to see her, but seriously, would anyone let them on a working barge bound for Memphis with Luana looking like that?

Luana looked around her and smiled.

"Aah," she sighed, "early Giza—a good choice, Musa. Let's see if the gods will bless or curse us on our journey."

"We've certainly had mixed fortunes so far." Musa told Luana about the rich person who had died from cholera, and the totally cool Khemten.

"Well, I'm feeling lucky, so let's see if the captain will let us aboard his barge for the trip toward Memphis."

The captain received her enthusiastically: "Your ladyship is most welcome aboard," he said.

"Come, my servants!" commanded Luana in her most regal-sounding voice.

Musa hurried aboard, but Seth lingered, watching the sailors hoist the square papyrus sail high on its mast.

"Hurry up, Seth!" Musa shouted.

"SETH?" cried the captain and crew.

"No way! You're not coming aboard *my* barge. I'm not superstitious or anything, but anyone who shares a name with the god of violence doesn't get on my ship!"

"But... but he saved Mau," pleaded Musa. "What about the blessings of Sekhmet?"

"I'm sure your friend's noble act will help him in his afterlife, when his good and bad deeds are weighed up by the great god Anubis, but get real, will you? Look out on the water! Do you think all those boats are friendly? Ever heard of pirates? Now, they're a *real* curse," the captain replied.

Seth froze as two oarsmen steered the barge quickly into open water, soon slipping smoothly upstream. Musa and Luana clung to the stern of the boat, watching Seth get smaller and smaller.

"I'm cursed!" he yelled.

"I thought you were an app expert. Think of something!" called out Musa.

Seth tried not to sound exasperated.

"I haaaave!" he bawled. "I've reset the coordinates on the app, and I'm now programmed to meet you in Memphis. There's no way I'm going to try landing on a moving barge! It's really annoying—I'll miss the river trip!"

His SLIP-mates could no longer hear him.

Runway Rundown

White is the color to wear this season: the catwalk at Giza Fashion Week was a sea of draped white linen and cotton for both men and women. As always, wigs were the headgear of choice for the designers showing at Giza.

▶ Ramesses I and Anubis are on trend with their armbands and wristbands.

This season, it's all about gold jewelry, whether it's plain or adorned with precious gems. Your outfit won't be complete without a gold necklace, bracelet, or ring.

▲Ramesses II's headdress lets everyone know who is in charge.

Amenirdis's wig and crown combo give her outfit a regal touch.

◀Our lord Amun looks chic in his simple schenti, or men's skirt.

▲The tight pleats on this dress, or kalasiris, really give it volume.

▶Queen Nefertari and Isis model loose- and tight-fitting styles.

43

THE MYTH OF OSIRIS

A popular myth from ancient Egypt narrates the story of a tragic rivalry between two divine brothers, Osiris and Seth. The myth was well known because the story of the death and revival of Osiris gave people hope of an afterlife.

Osiris was the son of the sky goddess Nut and her husband, the earth god Geb. He became the king of Egypt and ruled wisely with his wife Isis, establishing laws and teaching the people how to grow food and how to worship gods.

Osiris had only one enemy: his jealous brother, Seth. Seth secretly measured Osiris's body and made a painted coffin to fit it exactly. He then gave a feast, to which he invited his brother.

He showed off the magnificent coffin and said that he would give it as a present to whomever could fit inside it.

All the guests took turns lying down in the coffin, but they were all too small. At last, Osiris himself lay down, and his body fit perfectly. At that moment, Seth nailed the lid down, poured boiling lead over it to seal it, and set the coffin adrift on the Nile River.

When Isis heard what had happened to her husband, she was stricken with grief. She cut off her long hair, dressed in mourning, and set off in search of the coffin. Isis rescued the corpse, but when Seth found it, he cut it up and scattered the pieces all over Egypt. Sorrowfully, Isis and her sister Nepthys collected every piece. With the help of Anubis (the guide of souls to the underworld), Thoth (the gods' scribe), and Horus (Isis and Osiris's son), Isis and Nepthys pieced Osiris back together as the very first mummy. Isis transformed herself into a bird and, hovering over the body, she fanned life into it with her wings.

Osiris left the land of the living to rule the underworld, the land of the dead, where he judges the people's souls. However, when his son Horus grew to adulthood, Osiris briefly returned to ask him to avenge his death. In this way, Horus and Seth began their eternal struggle of good and evil. Sometimes one seems to win and sometimes the other, but neither can be vanquished. It is said that when Horus finally overcomes Seth, Osiris will return to the land of the living to rule as king once again.

CHAPTER 3

THE CURSE OF THE NILE

The trip to Memphis would take several hours. The barge glided smoothly through the water with surprising speed. It was already midday by the time they departed,

and the captain was determined to travel a good distance during the daylight.

Luana and Musa made the most of their short journey, taking in the scenes on both sides of the Nile. Just half an hour after their departure, they moored at a landing stage near a small settlement on the west bank, where important-looking officials stepped ashore. A scribe carrying several scrolls of papyrus under one arm and a box of writing tools under the other hurried behind them.

"They're probably land surveyors," said Musa. "They'll measure the extent of the flood, as they do every year." Remembering the flooded garden, he added, "This one's going to be a record, I think!"

The boat left the dock and continued on its way. Beyond the settlement, set higher than the river, the waters had receded, and the land was ready to be farmed. In the distant fields, oxen dragged wooden plows with sharpened bronze blades through the soil, made dark and fertile by the silt washed down during Akhet, the flood season. Farm workers hauled sacks of seed to scatter up and down the field, firmed in by the oxen's feet. The smell of freshly dug earth wafted toward the river.

"In a few months, it will be time for the harvest," the captain of the barge declared contentedly as he surveyed the scene.

"Looks as though there will be plenty of good barley for the beer..."

At the mention of beer, the crew shouted, "Waaaay!" but stopped short as a flotilla of boats threatened to push them into the riverbank.

"YEH!" cried the captain angrily, unsheathing a long knife and shaking it at them.

"The king's fleet," observed a man dressed in a very fine, pleated blue loincloth, leather sandals, and gold jewelry studded with sparkling gems.

"Judging by his clothes, he must be a merchant," Musa muttered to Luana.

"Not to be messed with," the merchant said as he shook his head at the captain of their barge. "Reckless young man! In all honesty, I'd rather be bound for Lebanon and all its riches on a sturdy sea vessel with the eyes of Wadjet painted on it for protection. These river barges make me nervous. They say that sailors and merchants are blessed on a ship, but I know plenty who've been cursed by bad luck."

Musa looked at Luana in alarm. Luana said, "Well, we might not be sailors or merchants, but we do have the eyes of

Wadjet to protect us. Look!" She pointed
to the turquoise amulet of the protectress
of Egypt, strung around her neck.

"It's just as well! The captain's steering
us into the reeds!" said Musa in alarm.

"A necessary move," observed the
merchant. "I knew the captain would submit
to the king's fleet in the end. At least the
cargo's safe. That's all I care about."

The scene in the reed beds was serene and pretty, with clumps of sturdy bulrushes and pink and white lotus flowers floating in between the reeds. Washerwomen were standing by the edge of the river with their piles of white linen clothes, frothing with natron soap, while fishermen with string lines were dipping into the water. Every now and then, someone would yell, "Crocodile!" and the workers by the waters would grab their goods and scramble up the banks. It all seemed so peaceful.

BANG! The barge lurched forward as a boat rammed it from the side.

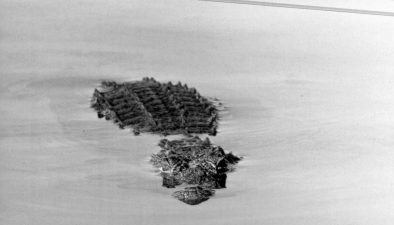

"Pirates!" yelled the captain as a horde of Nile bandits crashed into the barge and jumped aboard. The pirate captain slashed his way through the frantic ships' crew looking for booty. Then he spotted Luana in the distance and, seeing her expensive clothing and jewelry, thought he'd hit the jackpot. He made straight for her.

"Aaah, Wadjet!" he cried, pointing to the amulet around Luana's throat. "She is the goddess of the fifth hour of the fifth day and destroyer of the enemies of the dead! This shall be my lucky charm."

The pirate lunged at Luana. Realizing what he was after, she quickly ripped off her amulet and threw it at his face, yelling, "Take it, and leave me alone!"

At the same time, Musa picked up a rough block of granite he had found and launched it onto his shins.

"Run for the stern!" yelled the captain to Luana and Musa.

Luana and Musa dashed to the back of the barge, squeezing between stacks of barley baskets, well out of sight.

"We have to get out of here," Luana whispered, out of breath. Together, Musa and Luana took their cell phones out from their hiding places. Silently, they both knew they had to SLIP.

"Hey! D'you know something, Luana?" said Musa solemnly. "Maybe Seth's right. Maybe we are cursed! I'm not sure I really want to see the tombs at Dahshur."

"Don't be silly! Of course you do," Luana replied.

"That's the whole reason we came back to ancient Egypt, and we can't let some silly pirates get in our way." Then, without truly believing it, she added firmly, "They've stolen the amulet of the goddess of truth and justice. It is they who will be cursed! Ready to SLIP?"

"More than ready! Let's go!"

5-4-3-2-1. Star key—pound-pound-pound...

THE ANIMALS OF THE NILE

The Nile Valley possesses a varied fauna, with a range of animals including mammals, birds, amphibians, and insects. Here are a few to look out for.

NILE CROCODILE

Crocodylus niloticus

The Nile crocodile has long jaws with exposed teeth. It feeds on fish, antelopes, zebras, and buffaloes, leaping up to pull drinking animals into the water. To the Egyptians, it represented the god Sobek.

LENGTH: 16 ft (5 m), max 20 ft (6 m)
WEIGHT: 500 lb (225 kg)
LOCATION: Africa, west Madagascar

HIPPOPOTAMUS

Hippopotamus amphibus

Despite its size, the hippopotamus swims under water with grace and trots at surprising speed on land. The male hippopotamus was feared in ancient Egypt, as it was associated with the god Seth and because it could overturn a boat.

LENGTH: 9 ft (2.7 m)
WEIGHT: 1½ tons (1.5 metric tons)
LOCATION: Africa

SACRED SCARAB

Scarabaeus sacer

In ancient Egypt, the scarab beetle symbolized the sun god Khepri. The real insect is large and pushes balls of dung around, which it buries, and in which it lays eggs. The Egyptians imagined that the sun moved in a similar way.

LENGTH: 0.08–6.7 in. (0.2–17 cm)
WEIGHT: up to 3.5 oz (100 g)
HABITAT: southern Europe, North Africa and western Asia

SACRED IBIS

Threskiornis aethiopicus

This white bird, with its black, featherless head and neck, was sacred to the god Thoth and revered in ancient Egypt. It lives easily with people and consumes a variety of foods, including garbage, insects, and aquatic animals.

LENGTH: 26–35 in. (65–89 cm)
WEIGHT: 3¼ lb (1.5 kg)
LOCATION: Africa (south of Sahara), Madagascar, Aldabra Island, western Asia

PEREGRINE FALCON

Falco peregrinus

The peregrine falcon is one of the world's fastest birds. It attacks animals in a steep dive, during which it may reach a speed of 145 mph (230 kph). In ancient Egypt, it became associated with the sky god Horus.

LENGTH: 13½–20 in. (34–50 cm)
WEIGHT: 1¼–3¼ lb (0.5–1.5 kg)
LOCATION: worldwide (except Antarctica)

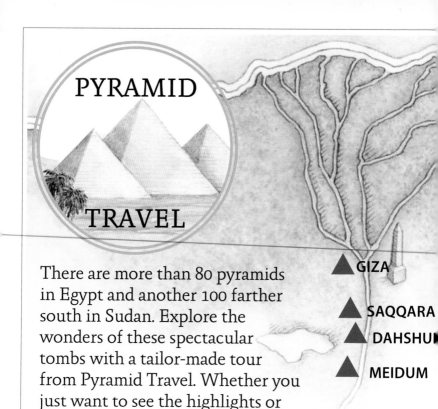

PYRAMID

TRAVEL

There are more than 80 pyramids in Egypt and another 100 farther south in Sudan. Explore the wonders of these spectacular tombs with a tailor-made tour from Pyramid Travel. Whether you just want to see the highlights or fancy yourself a true Egyptologist, we have a tour for you.

▲ GIZA

▲ SAQQARA

▲ DAHSHU[R]

▲ MEIDUM

Great Pyramid of Giza

The Great Pyramid of Giza was built for King Khufu around 2550BCE. Tourists have come to marvel at it for more than 4,500 years. Until the 19th century, it was the tallest building in the world.

Step Pyramid, Saqqara

This remarkable structure is the centerpiece of the vast Saqqara burial site. It was built for King Djoser by the high priest Imhotep in the 27th century BCE and is recognized as Egypt's first stone pyramid.

Bent Pyramid, Dahshur

Built by King Snefru in about 2600BCE, the Bent Pyramid is considered Egypt's first "true" pyramid because it has smooth sides, rather than steps. The bent shape may have come about to prevent cracking during construction.

Red Pyramid, Dahshur

Not happy with his Bent Pyramid, King Snefru began construction of the Red Pyramid—so called because of its ancient red graffiti—a few years later. It is second in size only to the Great Pyramid.

Meidum Pyramid

The Meidum Pyramid rises like a tower against the desert landscape. Only the inner core is left, surrounded by a pile of rubble. This was the first pyramid built by King Snefru, and it may have been started by an earlier king.

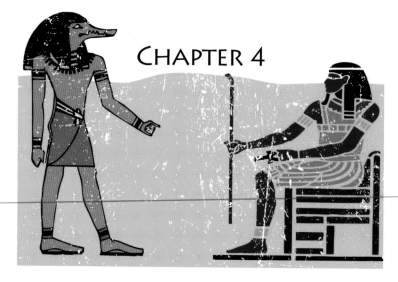

CHAPTER 4

THE CURSE OF THE POOR

HUMPH! Musa and Luana landed side-by-side on a mound of huge baskets of wheat, just offloaded onto the quayside at Memphis. All around, traders haggled loudly for the goods piled high along the dock: cedar and scented woods from Lebanon and East Africa, copper and turquoise from Sinai, cattle from Nubia, pink and gray granite from Aswan, and tin from Syria.

Musa and Luana jumped down from the pile of baskets and stared at the bustling, chaotic scene.

"Yeh!" yelled a voice from behind, making them jump. Their nerves were still shaken from the pirate attack.

"You're early!" It was Seth.

"Oh, it's you!" said Musa, breathing fast. "We've had quite an adventure…"

"My lady!" a voice interrupted from a nearby barge.

"Yes," replied Luana, as if she had been called "my lady" all her life. "What is it I can do for you?"

"I believe you are here to collect the consignment of perfume ingredients for the royal household."

"Why, of course. You've hired donkeys for me, I trust?"

"Certainly, my lady. I see you have servants to load and lead the beasts, and my man here will guard you."

"Typical! More work with donkeys!" Seth protested.

A cloud of intoxicating perfume soon shrouded the quayside as Musa and Seth loaded sticks of sandalwood, cinnamon, and pine, and petals of rose, jasmine, iris, and lily onto two huge baskets strapped on either side of each donkey's back. Then they were on their way, the guard leading them into the maze of tight backstreets that hugged the quayside, his eyes swiveling constantly and suspiciously.

The afternoon sun shone a golden glow on the red-brick buildings and the red earth beneath their feet. The noise of traders and

artisans pulsed in their ears. A coppersmith was beating out his molten metal, shaping it into tools, bowls, and figurines, and then coloring them with yellow and red, or silver and black. All the time, the heat of his furnace was driving passers-by tight against the opposite wall.

The donkeys were flicking their ears to create a little breeze around their sweating, fly-ridden heads. A barber with his pottery basin, perfumed soap, and brass shaving tools tucked under his arm was crying, "Gentlemen! Anyone for a shave? Latest soap fragrance available! Or a hair cut? Long back and sides, just as you like it!" Street-food sellers were hawking warm bread, honey cake, dried figs and dates, tiger nuts, and juicy berries.

Dancers with drums and cymbals were entertaining the streams of merchants and hawkers. Their bright ribbons and shiny metal beads floated around their arms and necks. Then, suddenly, they stopped. Behind Luana's perfume train, the slow beat of wooden clappers heralded a procession of mourners. Two bodies, shrouded in aromatic white linen and borne on a wood-and-wicker bier, were being carried solemnly toward the west of the city.

"May Ptah bless you. May he bless you evermore and into the life beyond," muttered the guard repeatedly and respectfully as the funeral party passed by.

"Where's all the bling?" Seth asked Luana, remembering the elaborate funeral back in the flooded garden.

"These bodies are the dead of the poor. They don't have riverside ceremonies or grand tombs. Their bodies are going toward the desert and the setting sun, not the rising sun of reincarnation to the east, as rich people's dead folk do."

"They'll be buried in the sand," added Musa. "My dad's found tons of them. They're covered in stones to stop the vultures and wild dogs from picking at the bones."

"Look!" said Luana, pointing westward. "You can see where they're heading."

The sad procession was nearing the edge of the town, and the scene beyond it to the west made them gasp.

"Tombs! Just acres and acres of tombs in the distance," Musa cried, "and beyond that, the rock burials of the poor. It means that back home, I'm probably stepping on people's remains all the time!"

"Exactly," Luana agreed, "and have you ever been cursed by it?"

"No!" laughed Musa. "I can't wait to go and examine them."

The guard stopped suddenly and ushered Luana into the royal perfume factory. There, men stirred vats of sweet and spicy perfume blends that emitted an almost suffocating aroma.

Musa and Seth unloaded the raw ingredients, and the head perfumer handed Luana a precious alabaster bottle filled with one of the prince's favorite perfume blends. The guard guided Luana, Musa, and Seth to the palatial royal quarters, built of white limestone. Its outside walls were covered in painted and carved scenes of mighty battles, abundant harvests, and shiploads of expensive goods from foreign lands.

They were ushered through the entrance

and into a chamber surrounded by bright-blue, red, and gold frescoes. Luana, with the perfume bottle held reverently in her hand, turned to her two companions.

"Off to the kitchens with you!" she commanded loudly.

"You're so bossy!" whispered Seth angrily.

"Actually, I'm doing you a favor. You might get a chance to eat! I'll stay in the pamper parlor for a while—just to get my makeup refreshed. I like the look of that bright-green malachite eyeliner over there. All in the name of historical research, you understand. Then I'll SLIP off home. Good luck with the mission, and don't get cursed!"

Egyptian Makeup and Perfume

The Egyptians went to great lengths to adorn themselves with cosmetics, wigs, and perfume. Both men and women used eye paint because they thought it had magical powers.

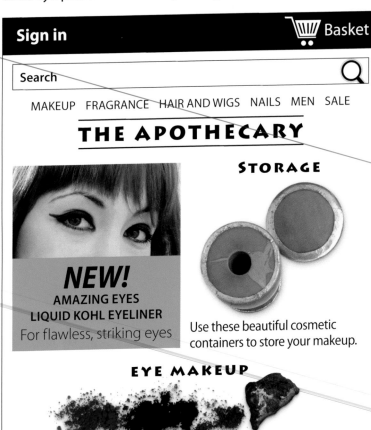

Sign in

Basket

Search

MAKEUP FRAGRANCE HAIR AND WIGS NAILS MEN SALE

THE APOTHECARY

STORAGE

NEW!
AMAZING EYES
LIQUID KOHL EYELINER
For flawless, striking eyes

Use these beautiful cosmetic containers to store your makeup.

EYE MAKEUP

Combine malachite (copper ore) or kohl (lead ore) and iron oxide pigments with water to make your own eye makeup.

APPLICATORS

Use these pigment applicators to scoop, mix, and apply makeup.

HAIR CARE

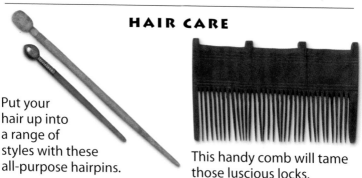

Put your hair up into a range of styles with these all-purpose hairpins.

This handy comb will tame those luscious locks.

Create lasting curls with this wig-curler (left), and pluck those stray eyebrow hairs with these tweezers (right).

FRAGRANCE

Perfume bottle

Sweet-smelling water lily is the perfect perfume ingredient.

Make your own perfume at home with this fragrant frankincense.

JOURNEY TO THE AFTERLIFE

An ancient Egyptian king has died. This is the beginning of the afterlife. The king must travel through the different levels of the underworld in order to reach eternal life in the Kingdom of Osiris.

STAGE 1: MUMMIFICATION

The king's organs are preserved, and the corpse is dried out. The body is perfumed and then bandaged with fine cloth.

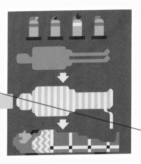

STAGE 2: INTO THE TOMB

The king's mummy is placed in a tomb. To ensure his comfort in the afterlife, the tomb is furnished with gold, jewels, slaves, food, furniture, clothing, wigs, perfumes, and all the luxuries befitting a king.

STAGE 3: ALIVE AGAIN

The king emerges alive in the underworld, home of terrifying monsters and dangerous beasts. He will not survive without the powerful magic in the Book of the Dead, which is buried in the tomb.

STAGE 4:
BOOK OF THE DEAD
To pass safely across the Lake of Fire and the demons, serpents, and crocodiles trying to thwart him, the king must chant hymns, recite spells, and follow all the instructions written in the Book of the Dead.

STAGE 5:
TESTED BY THE GODS
Gods challenge the king along the way. Here, Sekhmet delivers a tough quiz. Has the king been a good student? Does he know right from wrong? He can only advance to the next stage if he gets the answers right.

STAGE 6:
THE FINAL TEST
Anubis leads the king on to the final stage of the challenge. His heart will be placed on one side of the scales of justice. On the other side sits the feather of truth. Will his heart be pure and light, or heavy with bad deeds?

KINGDOM OF OSIRIS
Good news! Osiris has judged the king worthy of eternal life in the universe of the gods.

WINNER!

DEVOURER OF THE DEAD
Bad news. The feather of truth has deemed the king's heart too heavy with sin. His heart is thrown to Ammut, a creature part lion, crocodile, and hippopotamus.

GAME OVER

CHAPTER 5

THE CURSE OF THE CELEBRITY CHEF

"In the name of historical research!
I love that excuse!" Musa said, remembering
Luana's last words and shaking his head as
the guard led the way to the kitchen, set in
a baking-hot open courtyard.

The wonderful cooking smells felt like
torture. Bread, some savory and some
sweetened with honey and spices, was
baking in clay molds brushed with sesame

oil. A great pot of barley porridge steamed in one corner. There were lentils flavored with cumin in one, and with coriander in another. A delicious smell of cabbage, onion, and garlic filled the air.

"Yeh! You two! Come here and help!"

"I think that's the head chef," Musa whispered. "Let's not make his face look any redder and angrier than it does already."

The man, sweating from the heat of the work and the fires, pointed Musa and Seth to the charcoal store.

"You keep the fire going under that meat, okay? Read my lips, though—do not waste the charcoal! I know you poor kids—back home you just have a few pieces of animal dung and a couple of sticks of firewood. When you get in here, you think you can waste my expensive charcoal."

"We won't waste the charcoal, chef!"

"Hmmm. Good. You can turn the meat over as well. The goose cooks in its own fat—the chunks of hippo, too. You'll need to brush some sesame oil on the ostrich and the ibis, though. They're delicate. Oh, sprinkle them with a good fistful of salt,

some pepper, and some fenugreek, too—
they're in that dish over there. Normally,
I wouldn't be asking kids like you to help, but
we're preparing for a banquet and have some
inconsiderate dead guy in a mastaba to cook
for. Make sure you do it properly, okay? I've
won a Golden Gazelle award for my cooking,
and you'll be cursed if it's taken away!"

Seth and Musa looked at the meat and
then at each other.

"I've only ever seen a hippo in a zoo,"
said Seth.

"I'm wondering why the hippo-headed
goddess Tawaret doesn't curse anyone who
cooks it," added Musa.

"What's this mastaba thing?" Seth asked as he carefully oiled the ostrich.

"A kind of tomb. I really want to see inside one, since they usually have lots of spells and curses painted around the walls—at least, that's what Granddad says."

After an hour sweating over the fires, Musa got his wish.

"Okay, you two." It was the head chef speaking again. "You're going on a little journey. Don't get too excited. It's to a damp, smelly mastaba in Dahshur."

Musa tried not to smile.

"I've got food ready—a waste if you ask me. My sous-chefs are just wrapping it in papyrus. When you get there, spoon it out into the brass dishes, and leave them on the table. Then come straight back here."

He wagged his finger at them.

"Trust me. If you two so much as dip your fingers in that food, our great goddess Isis who nourishes us and blesses us with

a good harvest will be cursing you two into
an eternal hell of starvation. Got it?"

"Got it, chef!" shouted Musa and
Seth together.

"One more thing—you'll see a very large priest there. He's large because he takes all the food and wine home with him. He's sure to die young from his greed, but we're tired of it back here, where we sweat and toil. So you just report back to me if you see him stealing it."

"Will do, chef!"

The guard was ready with a donkey laden with food for the mastaba.

"C'mon," the guard urged the donkey. "C'MON!"

The donkey wouldn't budge, though, and Seth watched the shadows creeping across the palace.

"We're really cursed now," said Seth.

"YEEEEOOWWW!" A cat sprang, its claws outstretched, from the flat roof around the kitchen, scattering hundreds of raisins drying on mats in the late afternoon sun. It landed squarely on the donkey's head. The donkey brayed loudly, lurched forward, and trotted off so fast that the guard, Musa, and Seth had to chase after it.

"Sekhmet! We're blessed by Sekhmet!" chimed Musa and Seth gratefully.

According to the chef, who has been stealing food and wine from the tombs?

THE LOTUS FLOWER RESTAURANT

A trip to the Lotus Flower restaurant is truly a culinary experience. Our award-winning chef presents a menu of both Egyptian classics and innovative dishes.

❀ APPETIZERS ❀

Tilapia fish cakes

Seasonal salad topped with
seared duck slices

Baked goat and gourd parcels

Hippo paté served with date jam

❀ ENTRÉES ❀

Sautéed eel served with
garlic-infused lentils

Goose casserole flavored with fenugreek

Ostrich steak

Ox tongue in a red-wine sauce

❀ SIDES ❀

Seasonal salad of lettuce, cucumbers,
and pomegranates
Fresh baked bread from our own ovens
Couscous
Boiled barley

❀ DESSERTS ❀

Fruit salad of palm-tree fruit,
pomegranates, and melon
Dried fruit selection of dates, figs, and raisins
Date, almond, and honey cake
perfumed with rose water

❀ DRINKS ❀

Wine
Beer
Sheep or
goat milk

**WINNER OF THE
GOLDEN GAZELLE AWARD**

Egyptian Cat Facts

The ancient Egyptians had great respect for the animals that lived around them. Many animals were treated as gods, but no animal was more admired than the cat.

CAT GODS

Cats represented a number of different gods: the goddess Sekhmet (above) was often shown with a lioness's head, while the goddess Bast (right) had the head of a black cat. The sun god Ra was represented as a cat with rabbit ears when he fought the evil god of darkness, Apep, who was depicted as a serpent.

CAT MUMMIES

When cats died, some families took their beloved pets' bodies to the city of Bubastis, the center of worship for the goddess Bast. Here dead cats were embalmed, wrapped (right), and laid in cat-shaped coffins (below) before being buried in a cat cemetery.

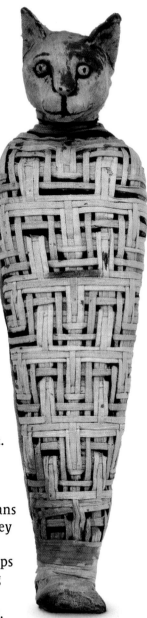

CAT FRIENDS

Ancient Egyptian records show that cats were kept as pets as early as 2100BCE. Today's domestic cats may be descended from ancient Egyptian pets. Cats were

valued by the Egyptians because they helped to protect crops by hunting mice, rats, and snakes.

THE CURSE
OF THE PRIEST

Walking toward the dipping sun, Musa
and Seth stared in awe at the mastabas and
pyramids in the distance.

Musa pointed to the southwest. "That's
the Bent Pyramid. You see how the angle of
the stonework changes halfway up? I can't
believe how new it looks, with its shiny
black granite top glowing in the sun!"

"Who's buried there?" Seth asked.

"No one knows."

"Stop here!" interrupted the guard, turning his head. "I'll leave you to unload. I've got to dash back to the port. King Snefru's ship is soon to drop anchor."

Musa and Seth pulled the donkey toward a low, flat-roofed building with sloping walls. Its heavy wooden door creaked open and, once inside, the musty smell of damp and chemicals hit their nostrils.

"Ugh! I don't think this is at all healthy," choked Seth.

"No. That may be why so many archaeologists in the past got sick," Musa replied. "There's mold and bacteria, and sometimes there's arsenic brushed over the walls."

"Arsenic?" exclaimed Seth.

"Yes, and natron salts, among other things. They're supposed to preserve the goods inside, as well as the paintings. Let's not stay too long!"

"Or we'll be cursed like the archaeologists?" Seth asked.

"No—poisoned. Maybe the archaeologists were, too."

They quickly laid out the offerings on the table—a flat block in the same shape as the mastaba itself.

"We've just got time to take a look at these amazing wall paintings," said Musa. "Ooh, and the hieroglyphs. Let's take pictures and send them off to Hiroto to translate."

Their phones flashed around the boldly written texts and the brightly painted scenes of fishermen, hunters, goldsmiths, weavers, priests, and gods.

BEEP! They had received a text message from Hiroto already.

"Hey u 2! Great stuff! U have lists of trade goods—gold, ivory, frankincense, etc. Stories of great battles & raids. Poems... wait 4 it... of death by crocodile, scorpion, snake, and the council of gods if u trash or steal from the mastaba...! There are your curses, Musa— just a list of threats."

Musa and Seth stopped reading as the door creaked open. They set about arranging the brass dishes on the offerings table.

"YEH!" yelled a very large man, clinking with gold and silver jewelry draped around his thick neck, arms, and waist.

"Get that food outside and onto my

donkey. Now! Or the war god Horus will strike you dead, and my guard here will help him!"

"NO!" shouted Musa and Seth together. "You're the terrible thieving priest!"

The guard lunged toward them with a long spear.

"We're CURSED!" bawled Seth.

"No, we're not!" Musa said as he turned around, grabbed a statue of a cat made of bronze, and threw it hard at the guard. Musa and Seth shot out of the mastaba, losing themselves in a maze of streets. They turned and looked at each other.

"SEKHMET!"

"Definitely time for the next part of our SLIP!" said Seth. "It was a hard piece of programming, so let's hope it works. Ready with your second SLIP?"

"Ready."

5-4-3-2-1. Star key—pound-pound-pound.

THUD! Musa and Seth landed on a huge wooden chest in the middle of a dark, silent space.

"Are we still in Dahshur?" Musa asked.

Seth checked their coordinates, relaying them to satellites in their own time.

"Yep. It worked!"

"Now we're in the next reign, though— King Khufu's, right?"

"Should be, if the instructions worked. Let's see if we can find out."

They switched on their cell phone flashlight apps and gazed around in awe.

"Wow! Where are we?" asked Seth.

"Some kind of tomb, I think—some kind of very fancy tomb," Musa replied. "It's new, too! After watching my dad unearth such old, broken, dusty stuff, I just can't believe how fresh and bright everything looks."

"And it doesn't smell too bad, either," said Seth, sniffing.

"No. They're definitely using a lot of chemicals. I can smell herbs and the perfume of sandalwood and myrrh, too."

They slid down from the chest. The room was full of pots and baskets. There were also boxes made of precious ebony and beautifully inlaid with colored woods. A low, ebony bedstead was encrusted with gold and green patterns, and twenty silver bracelets inlaid with turquoise, deep-blue lapis lazuli, and red carnelian shimmered.

Musa traced his fingers over the hieroglyphs on the wall.

"Spells, I think—to help the dead person into the afterlife. Look! Hiroto said this means 'Amun,' and it is with the symbol for the sun god, Ra. Amun-Ra—that's what the creator god later became, and I think…"

"Look over there!" cried Seth.

"A sarcophagus," Musa replied.

"Dare you peep in?" Seth asked.

"No. I don't dare, but I can take a good guess at who's inside. The thing is, Seth, I've seen some of this stuff before."

"Don't be stupid! We've never done a SLIP here before."

"No, back home. The bedstead, the box, the silver bracelets—they're in the museum in Cairo. This, Seth, must be the first tomb of Hetepheres, wife of King Snefru and mother of King Khufu. It's unbelievable! No one back home has ever found it!"

"Ooh, what's this?" interrupted Seth.

"It's a canopic jar. The museum's full of them, too."

"Canopic jar? Isn't that full of squishy internal organs, pulled out through the nostrils? Isn't that something they did during this time?"

"Mmmm. I'm definitely not looking in there! I wish I didn't believe in curses, but..."

"SHHHH! Voices!" warned Seth. A pile of stones crashed to the floor, and three men emerged, covered in dust. "Robbers!" gasped Seth. We're cursed... AGAIN!"

GIZA GAZETTE

FEBRUARY 13, 2570 BCE

OBITUARIES

Queen Hetepheres
2630 BCE–2570 BCE

Hetepheres, Queen of Egypt, King's Mother, Mother of the Dual King, Attendant of Horus, and Daughter to the God, died on February 6, 2570 BCE.

Even before her death, aged 60, her beauty, royal status, and devotion to her family combined to make her one of the most iconic figures of the 26th century BCE.

Soon after marrying Snefru, she became the most popular member of the royal family, and her death has created an outpouring of public grief.

Hetepheres was born on January 1, 2630 BCE, the daughter of King Huni and Queen Djefatnebti. She grew up in the royal household, largely out of the public eye until her marriage. Her sheltered upbringing did not stop her from growing up to be a kind and generous queen.

The royal family had been close to Snefru's for centuries. Hetepheres was seen as the perfect bride for Snefru, and they were married to great public acclaim in 2612 BCE. Their union confirmed Snefru's claim to the throne.

Their marriage was a happy one, Hetepheres being the model of a dutiful wife supporting her husband through widespread criticism of his wars and expensive building projects. Together they had eight sons and five daughters.

Her beauty was much admired both within the kingdom and abroad, and she is sure to be remembered as one of Egypt's most beautiful queens.

In her last days, she seemed satisfied with the life she had lived and with all of its achievements.

She passed away peacefully in her sleep on February 6, 2570BCE.

She will be buried in a tomb next to her husband, the late King Snefru, in Dahshur, along with several valuable items she will need in the afterlife.

She is survived by daughters Hetepheres, Nefertkau, Nefertnesu, Meritites, and Henutsen, and sons Ankhaf, Kanefer, Nefermaat, Netjeraperef, Rahotep, Ranefer, Iynefer, and our lord King Khufu.

GIZA GAZETTE
JANUARY 16, 2569BCE

OBITUARY ADDENDUM

Due to the malicious and greedy actions of grave robbers, it has been necessary to move the tomb of Queen Hetepheres, who died on February 6, 2570BCE, to a new location. Mourners should continue to pay their respects at her original tomb in Dahshur. Her full obituary was published in the February 13, 2570BCE edition of the *Giza Gazette*.

MERNEITH OF MEMPHIS
in Conversation with
KING KHUFU

MERNEITH: He may be our greatest king yet, but what does King Khufu really hope to achieve with his monumental building projects? We've been granted exclusive access to one of the world's most powerful men.

MERNEITH: When did you first decide to build a pyramid at Giza?

KHUFU: I've admired the great architect Imhotep ever since I was a young boy and first saw Djoser's Step Pyramid in Saqqara, which he designed. It's always been my dream to build a pyramid like that.

MERNEITH: Why have you and your predecessors chosen to build your tombs as pyramids, rather than in a more conventional mastaba shape?

KHUFU: The shape is designed to help me rise up toward the Sun in the afterlife, and the higher it is, the easier that will be!

MERNEITH: Some people have said that you were motivated to build the pyramid by a desire to outdo your father, King Snefru. How do you respond to this?

KHUFU: Well, it's more to do with making my transition toward the Sun as simple as possible. That being said, if I can build a pyramid that's taller than those built by my father, why shouldn't I?

MERNEITH: How did you feel when you finally saw the completed pyramid?

KHUFU: I was overwhelmed with pride in what we had achieved. I feel confident that when it is my time to leave this world, my body will be well protected inside.

MERNEITH: Your critics claim that the pyramid was built using forced labor. What do you have to say to them?

KHUFU: That is completely false. Everyone who worked on the pyramids was a free man and worked voluntarily on the project in order to honor his king.

MERNEITH: Your pyramid at Giza has been described as one of the wonders of the world. Do you think this honor is justified?

KHUFU: Only time will tell, but I think it will be a long time before anyone can build a structure anywhere near as marvelous as my pyramid.

MERNEITH: Would you like to comment on the recent scandal regarding the break-in at your mother Queen Hetepheres's tomb and the subsequent relocation of her grave goods?

KHUFU: I will only say that what happened showed a complete lack of respect for my mother, me, the rest of my family, and the Kingdom of Egypt. I vow to bring those responsible to justice!

MERNEITH: What do you expect your legacy will be?

KHUFU: I believe the pyramids we have built will inspire people to have hope that they, too, will be able to live forever in the afterlife.

HIEROGLYPHICS

The Egyptians had a kind of writing called hieroglyphics. Each hieroglyph, or symbol, stood for an object, sound, or letter. The French scholar Jean-François Champollion discovered how to read hieroglyphics using the Rosetta Stone in 1822. Here are a few hieroglyphics, along with the sounds that they make.

ROSETTA STONE
The Rosetta Stone was discovered in 1799.
It shows the same message written in three scripts: Egyptian hieroglyphs, Demotic, and ancient Greek. Jean-François Champollion could read Greek, so he looked for repeated words matched by repeated hieroglyphs.

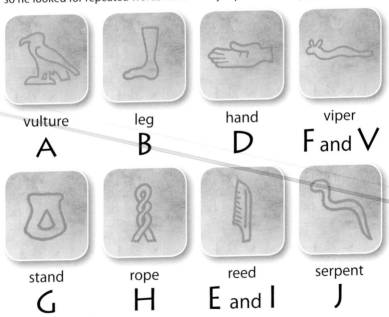

vulture
A

leg
B

hand
D

viper
F and V

stand
G

rope
H

reed
E and I

serpent
J

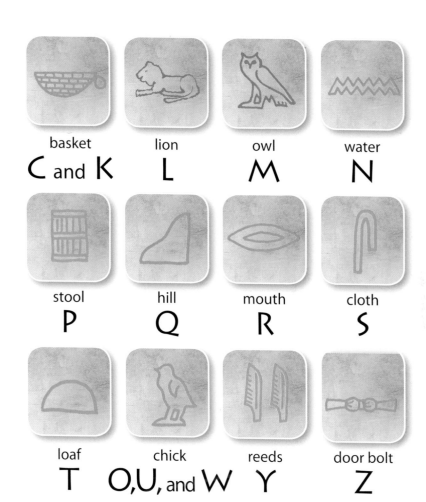

basket
C and **K**

lion
L

owl
M

water
N

stool
P

hill
Q

mouth
R

cloth
S

loaf
T

chick
O, U, and **W**

reeds
Y

door bolt
Z

CRACK THE CODE!

Can you decipher this word using the hieroglyphic alphabet?

CHAPTER 7

THE CURSE OF THE MUMMY

"Get them!" shouted one of the men, shocked at finding anyone in the sealed underground tomb.

Seth tapped on his cell phone, flashed its light into the robbers' eyes, and turned up the volume. His favorite band boomed and echoed chaotically.

"This is the curse of the gods!" he cried.

Yelling and screaming, the robbers scrambled up the rough, vertical shaft.

Musa and Seth
soon followed.

They tumbled out
into the cool darkness
and onto a steep
limestone step. Musa
looked around. It all
seemed strangely familiar.
A propped-up stone slab
covered the jagged robbers' entrance, and
a steamy, musty-smelling tunnel dipped down
steeply into the darkness from where they had
just emerged. Then he knew exactly where
he was, although the new archaeology site he
had left the day before seemed so, so far away.

"C'mon!" urged Seth. They walked away
from the robbers' entrance quickly—but
not quickly enough.

"Got you!"

Two soldiers, armed with spears and
wearing the emblem of Khufu's household
around their necks, grabbed Musa and Seth by
the arms and pushed them forward.

"What are you doing here? No one is allowed near this tomb! Are you robbing it?"

"You've got it all wrong!" cried Seth.

"Tell that to the king's priest!"

The soldiers marched them to a nearby temple, its towering stone statues of the gods lit up by rows of torches. At the entrance, a tall priest with amulets strung around his neck stared down at the two boys.

Musa looked puzzled. "Is he smiling?"

"Dunno. It's spooky," replied Seth.

The priest spoke solemnly. "So, you've been caught just outside our beloved Queen Hetepheres's tomb. Hmmm. Suspicious."

"But look!" pleaded Musa. "We have no stolen goods on us. We chased the robbers away, and we can show you their entrance."

The priest hesitated a moment, and then gave the guards their orders.

"Tell the king's vizier that there was an attempted robbery at his dear mother's resting place. I advise him to remove the grave goods and rebury them. Let her precious body remain there forever, untouched. By the way, these boys are not the robbers. You will have to mount a search for the real ones."

The priest removed two amulets from around his neck and turned to Musa and Seth.

"I strongly advise you to leave this place immediately. Before you go, take these as a blessing— and a souvenir."

Musa smiled as the priest offered him a lotus flower, a symbol of strength and a reminder of the Nile.

Seth gazed, puzzled, at his amulet. "It's an ankh, a symbol of everlasting life," whispered Musa.

Someone called out from inside the temple.
"High Priest Khemten!"
"Khemten? It can't be!" gasped Seth.

As they watched the priest walk away, they noticed something familiar—a twisted foot and a slight limp. Then they knew.

"It is! It's him, and he knew who we were, too!" said Seth. "He became King Khufu's priest. That's awesome!"

Musa clutched his amulet tightly. "Look, Seth, let's not push our luck any more. I think I know what I'm going to say about the curse of the mummies now, so should we just SLIP home?"

"Hold on," Seth replied, sniffing the air. "I can smell... CAKE!"

"Not NOW," Musa grumbled. "Anyway, how are you going to pay for it?"

Seth ambled over to the food seller, removed his amulet, and offered it for a very large slice of date, almond, and honey cake, perfumed with rose water.

"You can't do that!" Musa cried. "That amulet's priceless!"

"So's my stomach!"

"Oh, you're impossible! C'mon, let's SLIP."

"Do you want some cake?"

"NO! Ready?"

5-4-3-2-1. Star key—pound-pound-pound...

Musa was gone. Suddenly, Seth's greasy fingers lost their grip on his cell phone, and it slipped from his hands to the ground.

A guard dashed forward and picked it up.

"What's this? A stolen magic box? I knew it! We're returning it—and you—to the Queen's chamber to be locked up—forever!"

Seth's heart thumped like a drum as he was dragged back into the tomb.

"Seth! I am the mighty Seth! Feel my wrath!" a deep voice throbbed suddenly from Seth's cell phone. "I speak from the afterlife, and I'm telling you to let the boy go, or you'll be cursed!"

"Hiroto!" thought Seth. "He was listening in! He's saved me—again!"

The terrified guard pushed Seth away and ran for his life out of the tomb, dropping the cell phone. It shattered as it hit the ground.

Seth was alone in the dark and with no way home.

"I should have held on to my amulet. That Hetepheres mummy down there—she's truly cursed me!"

He slumped down onto the dusty ground. The night air blew a chilling breeze around his neck. Nearby, he heard a girl clear her throat. Seth lifted his head, squinted in the fading light, and then smiled with immense relief.

"Abrinet! I thought you were doing your exams! Oh, finally, I'm truly blessed!"

"Let's wait 'til we SLIP safely before you say that. Here, have my phone."

"How will you get back?"

"I've got my brother's. He said I could borrow it, although he obviously doesn't know it's gone 4,000 years away!"

"Then what? What will you do without your phone when we get back?"

Abrinet shrugged.

"Dunno. Never mind. Hiroto texted the alarm, and I was the only one who could get two phones, so c'mon—let's SLIP."

She looked all around at the shadowy tomb and shivered, more with excitement than fear.

"I think I just missed an awesome SLIP."

"You could say that. Together then..."

5-4-3-2-1. Star key—pound-pound-pound.

?
Who does Seth say has "cursed" him?

How to Make a Mummy

The Egyptians developed a method of drying a corpse with natron, a natural salt that left a body more flexible and lifelike than drying it with hot sand. If you would like to give it a try yourself, here is how to do it.

INGREDIENTS:

- natron (a type of salt)
- palm wine
- spices
- cedar oil
- wax
- gum
- linen bandages
- sand or sawdust
- 4 canopic jars
- selection of brain hooks
- flint ritual knife
- amulets

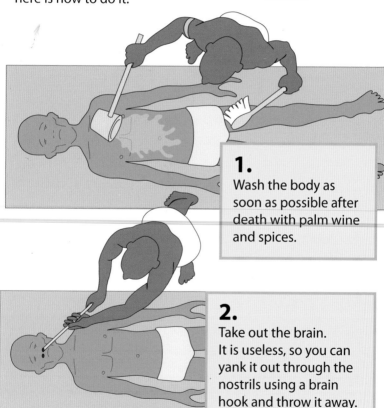

1.
Wash the body as soon as possible after death with palm wine and spices.

2.
Take out the brain. It is useless, so you can yank it out through the nostrils using a brain hook and throw it away.

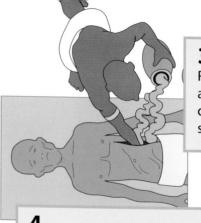

3.
Remove the internal organs and place them inside the canopic jars. Leave the heart, since it contains the soul.

4.
Fill the body with natron to absorb moisture. Cover the body with more natron, and leave it to dry for 40 days.

5.
Rub the skin with cedar oil, wax, and gum. Stuff sand or sawdust inside the body to give it shape, and put balls of linen into the eye sockets.

6.
Wrap the body in linen bandages, placing amulets between layers to protect the mummy on its journey to the afterlife.

WARNING!
Mummification should not be attempted on friends, family, or pets, or without adult supervision.

PYRAMID CONSTRUCTION

The pyramids are amazing achievements that involved enormous effort, time, and expense. They also needed very careful planning, with detailed drawings and calculations by skilled architects. This is their story.

PROD. *How They Built the Pyramids*

DIRECTOR *Imhotep*	CAMERAMAN *Ptahepses*
SLATE 128	**TAKE** 3

DATE *2609BCE*

SHOT 1
Camera: **long shot**

Workers quarry stone blocks by hammering wooden wedges into solid rock. Water poured over the wedges makes them swell and splits the rock.

SHOT 2
Camera: **long shot**

Blocks are hauled to the rising pyramid by sled.

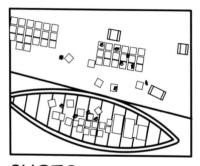

SHOT 3
Camera: **bird's-eye view**

Fine limestone for the outer casing is ferried from a quarry up the Nile by barge.

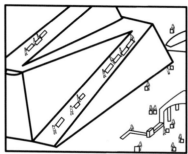

SHOT 4:
Camera: **extreme long shot**

Workers drag the blocks up the pyramid using a series of ramps spiraling around the pyramid.

SHOT 5:
Camera: **long shot**

The workers start to dismantle the ramps from the top down by breaking them up and hurling the pieces over the side.

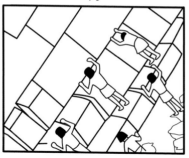

SHOT 6:
Camera: **long shot**

As they work their way down, stonemasons smooth the outer facing with copper chisels.

THE CURSE OF THE MUMMY

Rumors of Egyptian mummies' curses have been around for centuries. Yet no mummy has struck more fear into people's hearts than that of Tutankhamun.

The gold funerary mask of Tutankhamun

THE DISCOVERY

In 1922, archaeologist Howard Carter discovered the tomb of Tutankhamun, a young Egyptian king who had virtually been forgotten. The tomb was filled with priceless artifacts, along with the king's glittering sarcophagus, which contained his mummy.

Howard Carter beside the coffin of King Tutankhamun

THE CURSE

As soon as news got out about the discovery, rumors about the curse of the mummy spread. It was reported that the outside of the tomb bore the inscription, "Cursed be those that disturb the rest of the king."

Then a series of strange events was reported: first, a cobra, an animal said to protect Egyptian kings, ate Carter's pet canary. Lord Carnarvon, Carter's sponsor, died suddenly just a few weeks after the tomb was opened, and the entire city of Cairo was plunged into darkness in a sudden blackout. A number of other visitors to the tomb also suffered health problems or died.

Howard Carter *Lord Carnarvon*

THE TRUTH

No inscription about a curse has ever been found on Tutankhamun's tomb. Despite the troubles of some team members, out of the 58 people who were present when the tomb and sarcophagus were opened, only 8 died within 12 years. Carter himself did not die until 1969.

Most of the misfortunes blamed on the curse have rational explanations. Carter's pet canary had been left with a friend in England, so it could never have met a cobra in Egypt. Lord Carnarvon's death was actually caused by a mosquito bite that became infected, and blackouts were a regular occurrence in Cairo in the 1920s.

Is the curse fake? Many scientists believe that various harmful substances and organisms can be found in mummies and tombs, so disturbing a mummy may be dangerous, after all!

EPILOGUE

It was evening on the following day. Musa wandered through the cool Egyptian air over to the new archaeology site, where the dig was progressing slowly.

"Dad? Have you found out where the tunnel goes yet?" he asked.

"No. No clues so far, son. We obviously haven't reached the end of the tunnel yet, but everything seems to be stripped out." He shook his head rather gloomily.

Musa scuffed his sneaker in the sand, sat down on the deep limestone step, and suggested casually, "Ever thought it might be the robbers' tunnel to Hetepheres's first tomb?"

Musa's Dad and uncle looked at each other. One of the other archaeologists stared, wide-eyed, at Musa.

"Hetepheres!" the other archaeologist exclaimed. "I'd never even thought that we might find her mummy here!"

Musa was pleased—a great result from the SLIP. He hoped his competition entry would be, too.

Over in England, Seth had some explaining to do.

"Why are your arms and legs covered with black silt?" his mother wanted to know. How could Seth possibly explain?

Banished to his room to do his homework, Seth heard his cell phone beep.

"Hi Seth. How u doing?"

"Thought u had no cell!"

"Ah! Dad bought me a new 1 because I studied so hard."

"Did u know u'd get it b4 u rescued me?"

"Mm... maybe!" Abrinet smiled to herself and sent another text message.

"Anyway, c u, Musa, & Luana in Athens. Ancient Greek Festival of Thesmophoria. October 11, 09:00 hours GMT. U need 2 wear a classy tunic—and don't complain!"

Across the Atlantic, Luana wrote up her notes on the SLIP in her diary. She added a few more gods and goddesses to her database, and then sent it as an attachment to the other SLIP members. Luana filed it away in her mind, too.

The SLIP remained filed away in her mind until the following month. For on the fifth hour of the fifth day, the sacred hour of Wadjet, Luana awoke in the darkness and

gazed at the crescent moon. It reminded her of the shape of Wadjet's eye gazing down on her. She sensed a magnetic pull and a comforting magic all around her, and she felt strangely blessed.

THE MUMMY'S CURSE QUIZ

See if you can remember the answers to these questions about what you have read.

1. Why does Khemten tell Seth and Musa to stay away from the rich person's funeral procession?

2. What is the name of the Egyptian goddess with the head of a lioness?

3. Who is Mau?

4. Why do the dockworkers bow to Luana?

5. In the myth of Osiris, who murders Osiris?

6. With which god did the Egyptians associate the scarab beetle?

7. Which is the largest of the ancient Egyptian pyramids?

8. Why were cats so valued in ancient Egypt?

9. What is Musa's explanation for archaeologists entering the tomb getting sick?

10. What did the ancient Egyptians use natron salts for?

11. Whose tomb does Musa say they have found?

12. Queen Hetepheres was the mother of which Egyptian king?

13. How do Seth and Musa recognize the high priest as Khemten?

14. Why doesn't Seth SLIP back with Musa?

15. Who travels back to ancient Egypt to rescue Seth?

ANSWERS ON PAGE 125.

Glossary

Amulet
An object that is believed to bring luck or to have magical powers.

Bier
A stand on which a coffin rests.

Consignment
A batch of goods for delivery.

Fauna
The animal life of an area.

Flotilla
A group of boats.

GMT (Greenwich Mean Time)
The time in Greenwich, England, which is used as the standard for time-keeping across the world.

Inlaid
Decorated by inserting small pieces of material into an object.

Mastaba
A rectangular tomb with a flat roof.

Natron
A type of salt used by the ancient Egyptians to dry out a corpse during mummification.

Papyrus
A type of water plant that can be used to make paper, cloth, and building materials.

Prow
The front part of a ship.

Quayside
Next to the dock.

Resin
A material that comes from a plant and is used to make a kind of clear paint.

Reverently
Respectfully.

Sarcophagus
A stone coffin.

Scribe
A writer or secretary.

Silt
Solid material left by a body of water.

Sous-chef
A chef's assistant.

Stern
The back of a ship.

Triangle
A triangular drawing tool used for measuring angles.

ANSWERS TO THE MUMMY'S CURSE QUIZ:

1. The corpse is infected with cholera; **2.** Sekhmet; **3.** The cat that Seth rescues from the river; **4.** She is dressed like an Egyptian princess; **5.** His brother Seth; **6.** Khepri; **7.** The Great Pyramid of Giza; **8.** They helped to protect crops by hunting mice, rats, and snakes; **9.** Mold, bacteria, and arsenic are found in the tombs; **10.** To dry corpses out for mummification; **11.** Hetepheres; **12.** King Khufu; **13.** He has a twisted foot and a limp; **14.** He goes to by some cake and then drops his phone before he can SLIP; **15.** Abrinet.

Index

afterlife 40, 44, 45, 72–73, 94, 97–99, 109, 113
amulets 33, 51, 53, 55, 104, 106, 107, 110, 112, 113, 124
animals of the Nile 52, 56–57

Bast, *see* Wadjet

canopic jars 94, 95, 112, 113
Carnarvon, Lord 117
Carter, Howard 116, 117
cats 29, 34, 35, 81, 84–85, 90

fashion 18, 38, 42–43
flooding of the Nile 17–19, 21, 30–31, 47, 48, 66
food and cooking 32, 44, 64, 72, 74, 76–78, 80, 82–83, 90, 107

Hetepheres 94, 96–97, 99, 104, 110, 119
hieroglyphics 14, 89, 92, 100–101

Isis 29, 31, 43–45, 78

Khepri 33, 57, 125
Khufu 14, 58, 91, 94, 97–99, 103, 107

makeup 69–71
mastabas 77, 78, 80, 86, 89, 91, 98, 124
mummification 72, 112–113

natron 52, 88, 112, 113

Osiris 28, 31, 44–45, 72, 73

perfume 20, 62, 64, 67–72, 92, 107
pyramids, construction 59, 114–115
pyramids, important
Bent Pyramid, Dahshur 14, 59, 86
Great Pyramid of Giza 14, 58, 98–99
Red Pyramid, Dahshur 8, 59
Step Pyramid, Saqqara 59, 98

Rosetta stone 100

scarab beetle 33, 57
Sekhmet 29, 35, 39, 73, 81, 84, 91
Snefru 8, 9, 14, 59, 87, 94, 96–98

Tutankhamun 14, 116–117

underworld, *see* afterlife

Wadjet (or Wadjet-Bast, Bast) 29, 50, 51, 53, 84, 85, 121

About the Author

Catherine Chambers was born in South Australia and brought up in England. In college, Catherine studied for a degree in African History and Swahili. She loves books and worked in publishing as an editor. For the last 20 years, Catherine has written both fiction and nonfiction children's books. She really enjoys writing biographies and about history and geography—and likes to turn everything into a story. Catherine has lived in northern Nigeria and Portugal, as well as Britain. She has learned much from her travels and her three sons. Her other interests include trying to learn languages, visiting art galleries, and sipping coffee at King's Cross St. Pancras International train station in London, England.

About the Consultant

Dr. Linda Gambrell, Distinguished Professor of Education at Clemson University, has served as President of the National Reading Conference, the College Reading Association, and the International Reading Association. She is also reading consultant to the *DK Readers*.

Here are some other
DK Adventures you might enjoy.

Terrors of the Deep
Marine biologists Dom and Jake take their
deep-sea submersible down into the world's
deepest, darkest ocean trench, the Mariana Trench.

Horse Club
Emma is so excited—she is going to
horseback-riding camp with her older sister!

In the Shadow of the Volcano
Volcanologist Rosa Carelli and her son Carlo are caught up in
the dramatic events unfolding as Mount Vesuvius re-awakens.

Clash of the Gladiators
Travel back in time to ancient Rome, when gladiators
entertained the crowds. Will they be spared death?

Ballet Academy
Lucy follows her dream as she trains to be a professional
dancer at the Academy. Will she make it through?

Galactic Mission
Year 2098: planet Earth is dying. Five schoolchildren
embark on a life-or-death mission to the distant star
system of Alpha Centauri to find a new home.

Twister: A Terrifying Tale of Superstorms
Jeremy joins his cousins in Tornado Alley for
the vacation. To his surprise, he discovers they are
storm chasers and has the ride of his life!